A DAY TO REMEMBER

WORDS BY BERNARD STONE
ILLUSTRATIONS BY ANTON PIECK

MUSIC COMPOSED BY WALLACE SOUTHAM

THIS EDITION FIRST PUBLISHED IN GREAT BRITAIN 1981
BY ERNEST BENN LIMITED, 25 NEW STREET SQUARE, LONDON EC4A 3JA
AND SOVEREIGN WAY, TONBRIDGE KENT TN9 1RW
ILLUSTRATIONS © UITGEVERIJ OMNIBOEK, DEN HAAG 1981
MUSIC © WALLACE SOUTHAM 1981
TEXT © BERNARD STONE 1981
PRINTED IN HOLLAND
ISBN 0 510 00113 0

Ernest Benn
LONDON & TONBRIDGE

FOR SAMANTHA

ANTON PIECK

Anton Pieck was born in Den Helder, in Northern Holland on 19th April 1895. His family were not rich and they lived prudently. He grew up with a small circle of relations and friends and the occasional shopping trip to the nearest town was a tremendous event. Perhaps these things are reflected in the painstaking accuracy of his work, coupled with a child-like sense of wonder and excitement which has never left him. A toy shop at Christmas time, a travelling fair, are almost magical events.

His vision of life in the past is reassuring and enduring. He loves to draw old buildings and scenes from a time even before he was born. His illustrations are detailed and convincing; but there is always a sense of fairy-tale in his work. It is possible to imagine what the cupboards hold and to imagine the children playing around his many inviting corners.

This story is set in Holland in the nineteenth century.

There was an air of excitement and happiness in the city.
It was just before the feast of St. Nicholas. Christmas would soon be here.

Some people came from far and wide, many by canal-boat.

Some came to buy presents.

Others just to gaze in the colourful shop windows and enjoy the festivities.

Children were having a wonderful time. There were kites,
Chinese lanterns and toys in the sweet shop.
Martha, Jennie and Carl were so busy looking at everything they didn't notice the cat.

The grocery shop had a variety of good things to eat at this time of the year.

The children played all their favourite games.

Karen found time to give the milk seller's dog a drink of water.

Elsa loved going to the bookshop with her father. She was hoping he would buy her a book of fairy tales.

Young Theo watched the apothecary mixing herbs, whilst old Hans
was busily sharpening tools on his grindstone.

Eleanor was so intent on feeding the geese she didn't even notice her friend
Jemima looking out of the window.

The market-square had been turned into a fairground.
The acrobats by the village pump were a great attraction.
There were so many good things to buy; so many entertainments to watch.
So many old friends to meet.

The Punch and Judy man was blowing his trumpet so hard,
his eyes nearly popped out of his head.

Pepé the monkey was dressed in his new coat and hat,
but the crowds hurrying into the circus just passed him by.

But not everyone liked the music being played on the bandstand.

The merry-go-round with its flying horses, animals and chariots was very popular. Everyone wanted to have a ride.

In their houses neighbours met and talked about the year gone by.

When the river froze over it soon became a large ice-rink.
It was an opportunity for the skaters to see how skilful they were.
Quite a few people just couldn't keep their balance and fell down with
a resounding bump on the ice.

A makeshift tent had been put up and turned into a café.
Hot chocolate was especially welcome as the weather was bitterly cold.

A horse driven sleigh raced across the ice.
It was a most exhilarating way to ride and watch the skaters.

The baker went out on the ice with his sleigh full of tasty gingerbread.
His little daughter Berthe would sell them from her basket.

Hot water for the household was carried from the big steam furnace in the street.

A procession to herald the approach of St. Nicholas paraded through one part of the city.

In another district, St. Nicholas himself led the procession.

One elegant lady went by horse-drawn sleigh to buy all her presents.

Delicious hot bread rolls were bought for all the family.

At nightfall the musicians and singers went about the city entertaining the people on their way home.

Their favourite carol was called *The Christmas Message*.

'THE CHRISTMAS MESSAGE'

BERNARD STONE

T.W. SOUTHAM

It's the season of good ti — dings. And Christmas will soon be here. There's love, there's comfort, and bles-sings, As the church bells ring loud and clear. Don't for

get the poor and the lone — ly, The sick and the absent ones too, And the gent-le Lord will bless them all, Bringing gladness and happiness anew. When the

'day at last has en — ded, And the children are fast a — sleep, Once more think over what Christmas means, And its mes-sage for all to keep.

Frederick was the last to go home on Christmas eve.
He skated off in a jaunty manner. First on one leg and then on another.
Off he went, under the little bridge and away to his village.
It had been a marvellous day. A day to remember.